Long Lost Relatives

Written by George Ivanoff

Illustrated by Bruce Rankin

Published by
Sundance Publishing
One Beeman Road
P.O. Box 740
Northborough, MA 01532-0740
800-343-8204
www.sundancepub.com

First published 2002 by
Pearson Education Australia Pty. Limited
95 Coventry Street
South Melbourne 3205 Australia
Exclusive United States Distribution: Sundance Publishing

ISBN 0-7608-6740-2

Contents

Characters

Anna Cositas likes to help people. She also likes to use the Internet to find answers to her questions.

Marc Wealer is in Anna's computer class at school. He often acts like a know-it-all.

Chapter One

E-mail

Anna walked down the school hallway as fast as she could. She didn't want to be late. Usually her computer class wasn't one of her favorites. But for the past couple of weeks, they had been working on a special project.

Anna and the rest of her class were creating their very own web site. It had information about the kids in her class and their school.

They had learned about HyperText Markup Language (HTML) and how the World Wide Web and the Internet worked. Now they were able to e-mail kids at other schools, all over the world, who were doing similar projects.

Today was the last day they would be able to use class time to work on the web site. Anna wanted to scan some of the drawings she had done in art, her favorite subject. And then she was going to put them onto the school's web site.

She rushed into class only to find six other students waiting in line to use the scanner. Each of them had a folder stuffed with pictures and photos to be scanned. Anna sighed. Class would be over before it was Anna's turn to use the scanner. She'd have to find time to do it tomorrow.

She sat down in front of her computer and checked her e-mail instead. There were two new e-mail messages from Ikoku. She was a girl in Japan whose class was also making a web site.

Anna's eyes widened in interest as she noticed that there was a third message. She didn't recognize the name. The e-mail was from someone called Maria A., and the subject line read, "*Please Help!*" I don't even know a Maria A., Anna thought. What kind of help did this Maria need?

Chapter Two

Family Tree

Anna hurriedly clicked on the mystery e-mail message.

Hello Anna Cositas,

You do not know me. My name is Maria Andarkis, and I live in Greece. I would like you to help me find my grandfather's sister for a school project I am doing. I hope that this will be possible.

I found the web site you and your class did, and I noticed that you have a Greek name.

You also live in the same area where my grandfather's sister went to live. That is why I am writing to you. I do not know anyone else in your country. My school project is to do a family tree. I want to find out about my grandfather's sister, who came to your country many years ago. Can you help me?

I have been learning English. Does my English seem correct?

Thank you,

Maria

As Anna finished reading the message, she heard a sound behind her. She turned around to find Marc Wealer reading over her shoulder.

"Hey, that's my personal e-mail," she said, closing the message. "It's my business, not yours."

He smiled at her. "You don't even know this Maria person."

"That doesn't matter," Anna stated. "It was addressed to me. You shouldn't have been . . ."

"So, are you going to help her?" interrupted Marc.

"What?" Anna looked at him, startled.

"Are you going to help Maria find her long-lost relative?" Marc asked again.

"Well," Anna started to say, wondering why he cared. "I don't know. I wouldn't even know where to start," she said as she opened the message from Maria again.

"You can start by finding out more about the grandfather's sister, like her name." Marc pulled up a chair and sat down beside her. "Send Maria an e-mail and ask her. Then we can look the name up in the phone book."

"We?" asked Anna.

"Yeah," grinned Marc. "It sounds like an interesting mystery. I thought you might need some help."

Anna stared at him in surprise. Marc always liked to work on projects alone. And she had never seen him volunteer to help anyone else. Anna wondered if he was up to something.

"Why would you want to help me?" she asked suspiciously.

Marc shrugged his shoulders and walked away, blushing.

I wonder what's going on with him, Anna thought. Oh, well, she could use help. She was pretty sure that this search would not be an easy one.

Chapter Three

The Search

The next day, Anna and Marc met in the computer room at lunchtime. Anna was still surprised that Marc wanted to help, but she was glad to see him. He seemed happy to see her, too. They went and sat down at one of the computers. There was an e-mail message from Maria waiting for them.

"Great!" said Marc. "Maybe now we can get some more specific information on her missing relative."

Hello,

Thank you, Anna, for trying to help me. Please tell Marc I am glad he is helping me, too. The name of my grandfather's sister is Roula Andarkis. She left Greece in 1955 on a ship called Anestis *that landed near the area where you live.*

I cannot wait to hear from you again.

Thank you,

Maria

"Roula Andarkis," read Marc.

"Let's go to the library!" Anna said excitedly. She couldn't believe she was so willing to go into the library during lunchtime. Anna and Marc headed there and burst through the double door.

The school librarian glared at them. They quietly walked past the front desk, trying not to laugh.

"This way," whispered Anna to Marc.

The librarian rolled his eyes and sighed loudly. Then he buried his head back in the computer magazine he'd been reading.

Marc giggled the moment they were out of sight. "He's really a strange librarian, isn't he?"

Anna nodded, then went straight to the reference section and grabbed the local telephone directory. Finding the right page, she ran her finger along the names.

"Andarkis, R.," she murmured. "Only four of them."

She looked up at Marc. "That's two phone numbers each."

"Cool!" agreed Marc. "We can each call two of the numbers tonight from our houses. Then let's meet tomorrow morning to see if either of us found Roula."

The next morning, they met outside the school gate. Anna looked expectantly at Marc when he arrived. But he just shook his head slowly.

“Me, either,” sighed Anna. She kicked at the leaves on the sidewalk.

“Maybe Roula lives in a different area or state now,” suggested Marc. “We could go through the other phone books and make more phone calls.”

Anna laughed, then stopped when she saw the hurt look on Marc's face.

"I don't think our parents would let us make that many long-distance calls," she explained.

"I suppose not," Marc muttered under his breath as they walked slowly into the school. They didn't say anymore as they headed off to class.

Later that day in math class, Anna found a note on her desk.

Anna,

Got an idea. Meet me in the computer room after school.

Marc

Anna wondered what Marc had in mind. She could barely think about anything else for the rest of the day. She started counting the minutes until the bell rang.

Marc was already there when she rushed into the computer room.

"What?" she demanded. "What is it?"

"Roula's ship," he answered excitedly. "She was on a ship called the *Anestis* in 1955." He clicked on a link in the web browser. "I've just done a search for *Anestis* + 1955."

"And?" Anna leaned in to look over his shoulder.

"And," said Marc, "I think I've found something very interesting."

Chapter Four

Sea Voyage

Phyllis Braiden, Personal Memoirs, read Anna. "What's all that got to do with finding Roula?"

"Look at the chapter headings," said Marc, pointing to the third item on the list. "Voyage on the *Anestis*, 1955." He clicked on the link, and it took them to a long page of text. "I'll do a search for Roula on this page. Let's hope we find something."

Marc tapped away on the keyboard. A moment later they found a paragraph about Roula.

I met a lovely young Greek lady on the voyage. Her name was Roula, but I forget her last name. We spent some time together at the start of the voyage. She hardly spoke any English, so I tried to teach her as much as I could.

As the voyage progressed, I saw less of her, though, as she had met a handsome Greek gentleman. They had decided to get married by the end of the voyage. I'm afraid I don't remember his first name at all. I know his last name began with a C. They are both in the passenger photograph at the end of this chapter in the front row, holding hands. I'm in the second row, third from the left. . . .

Anna took Marc's place in the chair and scrolled down to the photo.

It was black and white, and very faded. But she could see Roula and the Greek man she was going to marry. Roula was very beautiful, Anna thought, with her long, dark hair and pretty eyes. She and the other passengers in the photo were standing in three rows. They were posing for the photograph on the deck of the ship.

To one side of them was a red and white life preserver with *Anestis* printed on it. Anna continued to stare at the photo. There was something about the photo. It looked familiar, she thought. Maybe she had seen it, or one like it, in a history book. She shook her head.

"So Roula would have changed her last name when she married this C guy," said Marc thoughtfully.

"That doesn't really help us much," sighed Anna.

"Oh, I don't know about that," said Marc with a grin.

"What do you mean?" Anna looked at him with a puzzled expression.

"Think about it." Marc was still smiling. "Your last name is Cositas, right?"

"Yes," said Anna.

"And Roula married a Greek guy whose last name began with C," said Marc.

Anna raised an eyebrow. "You mean you think that . . ."

"Well, it's possible, isn't it?" Marc looked hopefully at Anna.

"Don't be silly," Anna blurted out in disbelief. "Do you know how many Greek names begin with C?"

"Oh, yeah," Marc struggled to think of something to say. "But you never know. What was your grandmother's last name?"

“Ahhh . . .” Anna signed as she looked away, bothered. “I don’t know. She died before I was born. Mom and Dad always just called her my grandmother. They never told me her last name, but I know I have seen . . .”

Suddenly Anna stopped. It was like a lightbulb had been switched on in her mind. She now realized why the photo looked so familiar. Without another word, she bolted out of the classroom. Not knowing what to do, Marc got up and ran out the door after her.

Chapter Five

Finding Roula

Marc was out of breath by the time he ran up the driveway at Anna's house. He had barely managed to keep her in sight. He watched her race through the front door, leaving it open. He gave himself a few seconds to catch his breath, then went in. What had made Anna run off like that? Now at least he could ask her what was going on.

Marc found Anna in the living room, flipping through an old photo album. Several more albums were already lying across the floor.

"You know," he gasped, "you should be on the track team." Then he collapsed onto the sofa, exhausted, and looked over at her studying each photograph.

"It's here somewhere," said Anna, turning another page of photos. "I know I've seen it. I can feel it in my bones."

She finished with the photo album, tossed it to one side, and grabbed another album off the shelf.

"Aha!" she yelled after flipping over a couple of pages. "Here it is!"

"Here what is?" asked Marc, getting up from the sofa. He stood above her and looked down at the album.

She pointed to the old photograph.

Faded and torn around the edges, it was hard to see the faces of the people in it. Hard, but not impossible. And the life preserver with the name *Anestis* was clearly visible.

"It's the same photo!" Marc exclaimed, pointing at the album. "It's the photo from the web page."

"Yes," agreed Anna. "I thought it looked familiar when I first saw it. And then when you thought that Roula might be my grandmother, I remembered this photo."

"Wow!" Marc could hardly believe it. "All that stuff I said about Roula possibly being your grandmother was just a joke. I didn't really think that she *was* your grandmother. This is cool!"

Anna smiled at him and said, "It really is unbelievable."

"Let's take the photo out," said Marc.

Anna peeled back the plastic sheet in the album and picked up the photo. "I haven't looked through these photos in ages," Anna said, staring at the people on board the *Anestis*. She smiled at the photo, then gently returned it to the album.

Marc sat down beside Anna to look at the other photos. She turned the pages.

There were several photos of Roula. She had dark hair, large eyes, and a beautiful smile.

Marc looked from the photos to Anna. The two looked very similar, he thought, especially when Anna smiled. She definitely had her grandmother's beautiful smile.

"What are you staring at?" asked Anna.

"Ah . . ." Marc felt his cheeks burning. "Nothing. I was just thinking that you looked a bit like Roula."

Suddenly Anna jumped to her feet. "We've got to e-mail Maria!"

Chapter Six

New Relatives

Anna ran into the den to turn on her family's computer. Once again, Marc was several paces behind. She quickly opened the e-mail on the computer.

"You *really* should be on the track team," panted Marc. "I'm not kidding. You'd be great." He flopped down on the chair next to her by the computer.

Anna wasn't listening. She was too busy typing an e-mail message.

Hi Maria,

We found Roula! Well, actually we found out about her. I'm sorry to tell you that she died many years ago. But I've got some really exciting news for you.

Roula was my grandmother! Can you believe it? She changed her name from Andarkis to Cositas when she married my grandfather. They met when she came over on the ship Anestis. *This means that we're related! I think it makes us second cousins.*

So, you've got many more people to add to your family tree. There's me, and my mom and dad, and my brothers, George and Connor. Then there are my aunts and uncles and all of my cousins. You have lots of relatives here.

You'll have to tell me all about your family. (And I guess it's now my family, too!) Isn't this exciting?

Your long-lost relative,

Anna

Anna clicked the Send button and looked up to see Marc staring at her.

"Who knew that I would find a new relative because of a computer project," she said in amazement.

Then Anna smiled at him. "Thanks for all of your help."

Marc grinned back, then quickly turned away as his cheeks went red.

Anna couldn't help giggling as she suddenly realized why Marc had been helping her.

"Hey," she finally said. "It looks like I have a new relative—and a new friend!"